Peter Claus
and the Naughty List

Lawrence David   illustrated by Delphine Durand

A DOUBLEDAY BOOK FOR YOUNG READERS

For Russell Fitzpatrick
L.D.

For Bruno
D.D.

When the reindeer landed on Mitchell Plout's roof, Peter slid down the chimney.

FORT MITCHELL, a sign announced on a bedroom door. Peter quietly crept into the room and saw a snoring six-year-old boy. Peter shook him awake.

"Hey, who are you?" Mitchell asked.

"I'm Peter Claus, Santa's kid," Peter told him. "Did you know you're on the naughty list?"

"What naughty list?" Mitchell asked, rubbing his eyes.

"Santa's naughty list. I'm on it too."

Mitchell got out of bed. "I don't remember being bad this year."

Peter shook his head. "Nobody ever does."

"What can we do?" Mitchell asked.

"Come with me," Peter told him.

Peter gazed down at the land below. He saw mountains, oceans, valleys, and deserts. He saw a beautiful sunset in the west and a bright sunrise in the east. The world was so exciting and magnificent, he almost forgot why he was there. No one looked naughty from way up high. Peter took the list from his pocket. "Okay, reindeer, please go to Mitchell Plout's house," he said.

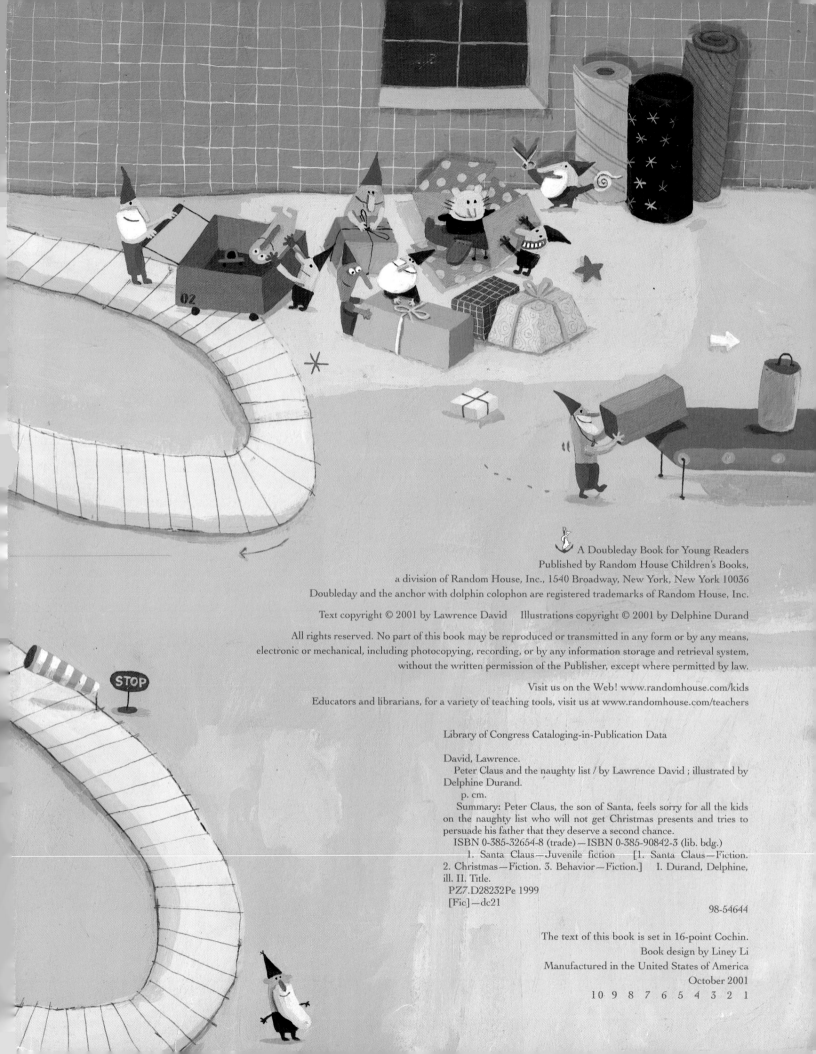

A Doubleday Book for Young Readers
Published by Random House Children's Books,
a division of Random House, Inc., 1540 Broadway, New York, New York 10036
Doubleday and the anchor with dolphin colophon are registered trademarks of Random House, Inc.

Text copyright © 2001 by Lawrence David   Illustrations copyright © 2001 by Delphine Durand

Visit us on the Web! www.randomhouse.com/kids
Educators and librarians, for a variety of teaching tools, visit us at www.randomhouse.com/teachers

Library of Congress Cataloging-in-Publication Data

David, Lawrence.
  Peter Claus and the naughty list / by Lawrence David ; illustrated by
Delphine Durand.
    p. cm.
  Summary: Peter Claus, the son of Santa, feels sorry for all the kids
on the naughty list who will not get Christmas presents and tries to
persuade his father that they deserve a second chance.
  ISBN 0-385-32654-8 (trade) — ISBN 0-385-90842-3 (lib. bdg.)
    1. Santa Claus—Juvenile fiction   [1. Santa Claus—Fiction.
2. Christmas—Fiction. 3. Behavior—Fiction.]   I. Durand, Delphine,
ill. II. Title.
  PZ7.D28232Pe 1999
  [Fic]—dc21
                                                                98-54644

The text of this book is set in 16-point Cochin.
Book design by Liney Li
Manufactured in the United States of America
October 2001
10 9 8 7 6 5 4 3 2 1

Naughty or nice?

Santa Claus, Mother Claus, and their son, Peter, were reading the letters the elves had delivered. "Another name added to the nice list," Santa told Peter as he wrote on a long scroll of paper. "Who's next?"

"Mitchell Plout," Peter said, opening a letter.

"How many naughties?" Santa asked.

Peter counted. "One hundred twenty-four."

"That's not so many for a whole year. How many nices?" Santa asked.

"One hundred twenty-three."

"Oh, well, write him on the naughty list," Santa said.

Late that night, Peter tiptoed downstairs and took the list of naughty names off Santa's desk. He sneaked out to the barn. The reindeer bleated happily as their friend entered.

"Do you want to go on a midnight mission?" Peter asked. "A lot of naughty children need our help." He hooked the reindeer up to the sleigh, climbed onto the seat, and gave a tug on the reins. One-two-three, the reindeer took off into the air, pulling the sleigh with Peter Claus behind them.

"Who's next?" Santa asked.

"Peter Claus," Peter said. He read the list of naughty things he had done during the past year. He'd yelled at his baby-sitter elf when he wouldn't let Peter stay up late and watch TV. . . . He'd forgotten to feed his pet reindeer one day and it had gotten sick. . . . He'd used the Christmas tree ornaments as bowling balls and had broken every last one. . . .

"How many nices?" Santa asked.

Peter counted seventy-four naughties and sixty-one nices.

Instead of answering his father, he just added his own name to the naughty list.

Peter looked at the naughty list. It was a short list, but Peter hated adding names to it. His own name had been on it the year before.

"Mitchell only had one more naughty than nice," Peter told his parents. "That doesn't seem fair."

"I didn't make the rules," Santa said. "But you know what they are: More nices than naughties and you go on the nice list and get lots of presents. More naughties than nices and you go on the naughty list and get nothing."

Peter remembered that there had been no gifts for him under the tree the past Christmas. He'd felt very sad. "Does it have to be that way?" he asked. "Can't naughty kids get gifts too?"

"Now, would that be fair to the good kids?" Mother Claus asked.

"That's the way my father taught me to do it when he was Santa, and the way his dad taught him," Santa said.

Peter wrote Mitchell Plout's name on the naughty list.

By morning the sleigh was filled with kids from the naughty list.
The reindeer pulled it high over the world. Peter asked the kids what
they'd done to be put on the naughty list.

They all had plenty of stories to tell.

The sleigh landed outside Peter's home. Santa and Mother Claus
bounded out the front door.

Peter stepped forward. "Hi, Mom and Dad."

Santa frowned. "Where were you?" he asked.

"We were worried," Mother Claus said. "Were you out playing on the sleigh all night?"

Peter held up the naughty list. "I needed to find these kids," he explained. "Don't you think you should find out why they did naughty things before you decide they belong on the naughty list? Isn't that the fair way?"

"Okay," Santa said with a smile. He gave Peter a pat on the head. "Mother Claus and I will take all you kids home and give each of you the chance to tell us why you were naughty."

"Then we'll get lots of presents?" one little girl asked.

"Well," Santa said, "I can't make it that easy. But if you tell me a good deed you'll do to make up for a naughty thing you did, maybe then you'll get some presents."

"Remember," Mother Claus instructed, "what's important at Christmas is giving to others. Show Santa and me that you know how to give and we'll take you off the naughty list."

The children jumped and cheered.

All the kids piled into the sleigh with the Claus family. The sleigh flew high above the clouds. Toby Malloy told Santa and Mother Claus that he'd called his sister Monkey Face.

Santa frowned. "Is that nice?"

"But she does have a monkey face," Toby said.

"You don't have to tell her that," Mother Claus said.

"Oh," Toby replied.

Santa landed the sleigh in Toby's backyard. Toby's sister was building a snowman, but the snowballs were heavy. Toby said he was sorry for calling her Monkey Face, and that he'd help her build her snowman.

"Okay," Toby's sister said.

Santa told Peter to take Toby's name off the naughty list.

The Claus family flew Betty Waddingwear home. She explained to Santa and Mother Claus that she had dressed her brother in toilet paper when he'd refused to wear any clothes. When they landed at her house, Betty told her little brother she wouldn't dress him in toilet paper again. "Next time I'll ask Dad to help me dress you," she said.

"And I'll let you help me better," her little brother promised.
Betty's father gave his daughter a kiss on the head.
Mother Claus told Peter to take Betty's name off the naughty list.

The Clauses flew Mitchell Plout home. Mitchell told them how he had hidden all his vegetables in his mother's shoes so he wouldn't have to eat them. When they went into Mitchell's living room, Mrs. Plout was decorating the Christmas tree.

Mitchell told his mom he was sorry and said he'd never put vegetables in her shoes again. Next time he'd either eat them or hide them in his pockets.

"Maybe I should just give you french fries," Mrs. Plout said.

"Anything more?" Santa asked.

Mitchell whispered in Santa's ear, "For her Christmas present, I'm going to give her a bouquet of carrots, broccoli, and radishes."

"Good boy," Santa said. He told Peter to take Mitchell's name off the naughty list.

After all the kids had been dropped off, the Claus family returned to the North Pole. The elves came out of the workshop and loaded the sleigh for that night's deliveries. Mother Claus went inside to make sure all the gifts were wrapped.

Santa *ho-ho-ho*ed. "It feels nice to have helped those kids do good deeds. We'll bring them presents now."

"Isn't there still one name left on the list?" Peter asked.

"Oh," Santa said. "Who could that be?"

"Me, that's who." Peter frowned. "Why is it so hard for me to be a good boy?" he asked. "Why can't I do nice things?"

Santa sat on a log and lifted Peter onto his knee. Peter watched as his father crossed the name *Peter Claus* off the naughty list.

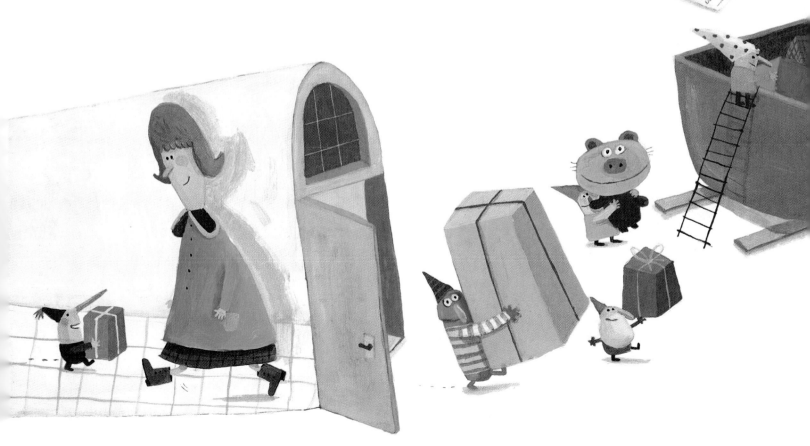

"But I didn't tell you how I was going to do something nice for someone," Peter said.

Santa nodded. "Ah, Peter, don't you see? You've helped all the children from the naughty list *and* their families. That shows me what a nice boy I have."

"Really?" Peter asked.

"You're always a nice boy, even when you do naughty things." Santa lifted Peter from his lap onto his shoulders. "Now let's head home for dinner."

"Dad?" Peter asked. "How come I do naughty things if I'm a nice boy?"

"All people do naughty things once in a while. It can't be helped," Santa explained. "Saying you're sorry is what matters most."

"Can we help all the kids on the naughty list every year?" Peter asked.

Santa *ho-ho-ho*ed. "That's a splendid idea. I can see you're going to make a great Santa when you're older."

Peter gave his father a pat on the head. "I want to be a Santa just like you."

On Christmas Eve, the children of the world slept snugly in their beds, except for one little boy named Peter Claus.

Peter was allowed to stay up especially late that night because he was riding in a sleigh piled high with gifts for the nice children of the world. Thanks to Peter, the list of nice children was especially long that year.

Santa *ho-ho-ho*ed. "I don't see any naughty kids tonight," he laughed.

"None at all anywhere," Mother Claus said happily.

Peter held the list of kids tightly in his hand. There was his name, right at the top: *Peter Claus*. A nice kid.

"Nope, I guess not," Peter told his parents. He smiled a broad smile. "Ho ho ho," he yelled to the stars.

"Ho ho ho ho ho," the Claus family cheered to all the children of the world. "Have a merry, merry Christmas!"